anything

D0938060

Zoomer's Out-of-This-World Christmas

NED YOUNG

Zoomer's Out-of-This-World Christmas

HARPER
An Imprint of HarperCollinsPublishers

Zoomer's Out-of-This-World Christmas
Copyright © 2013 by Ned Young

All rights reserved. Manufactured in China.
No part of this book may be used or reproduced in any manner whatsoever without written permission except in the case of brief quotations embodied in critical articles and reviews. For information address HarperCollins Children's Books, a division of HarperCollins Publishers, 10 East 53rd Street, New York, NY 10022.
www.harpercollinschildrens.com

Library of Congress Cataloging-in-Publication Data is available.
ISBN 978-0-06-199959-8 (trade bdg.) — ISBN 978-0-06-199960-4 (lib. bdg.)

Typography by Dana Fritts
13 14 15 16 17 SCP 10 9 8 7 6 5 4 3 2 1
❖ First Edition

For their out-of-this-world book-building skills,
a galaxy-sized thank-you to
Maria Modugno and Dana Fritts

For all my wonderful relatives
who filled my childhood memories
of Christmas with magic

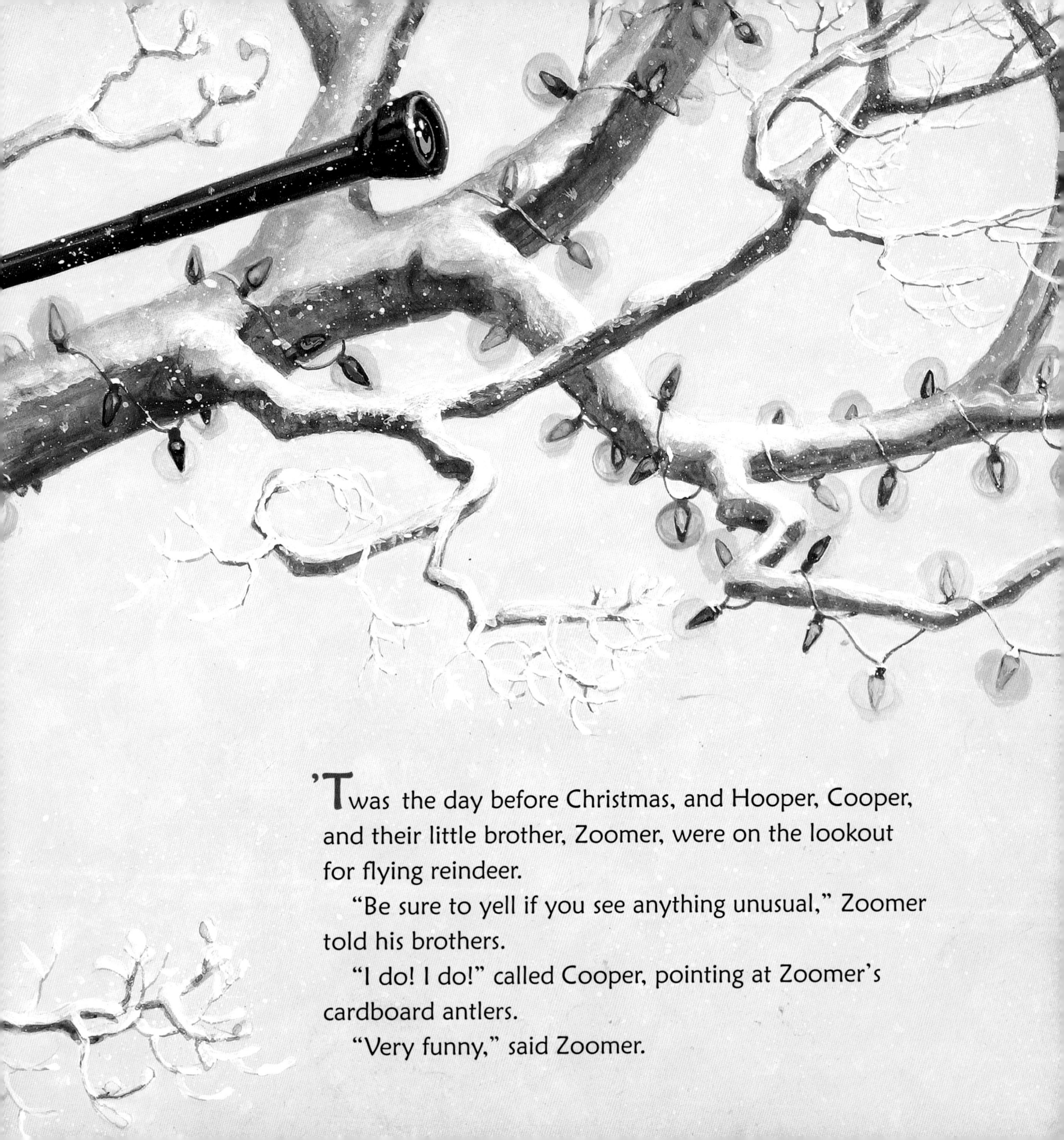

'Twas the day before Christmas, and Hooper, Cooper, and their little brother, Zoomer, were on the lookout for flying reindeer.

"Be sure to yell if you see anything unusual," Zoomer told his brothers.

"I do! I do!" called Cooper, pointing at Zoomer's cardboard antlers.

"Very funny," said Zoomer.

"Stop goofing around," yelled Hooper. "This could be it! Something is coming this way, and it's coming in fast—really, *really* fast!"

The pups all ducked for cover as the *something* shot past them and landed with a loud BOOM in the backyard.

"Boys!" called Dad. "What's all the noise about?"

"I'm not sure," answered Zoomer, "but I think Santa just landed in the backyard!"

"*Zoomer!*" Dad chuckled. "Where does he come up with this stuff?"

But as the pups reached the backyard, they soon realized . . .

. . . it *wasn't* Santa.

"Wowww," whispered Cooper. "What do you think it is?"

Before they had time to wonder, the spaceship's door slowly began to open. . . .

. . . And out stepped a family from outer space, their robot, and their pet—a yarple-headed gigantaziller.

"Welcome to our backyard," said Zoomer with a bow.

they replied with friendly smiles.

Then the space family invited Zoomer and his brothers to share their picnic.

They feasted on ***kookaloon*** sandwiches, ***zablookee*** salad, and ***blopwopple*** pie and washed it all down with some ***zoinkinfizz*** soda. Everything was *out-of-this-world* delicious.

After their meal, the space kids taught Zoomer and his brothers how to play

zlammaroo.

It was a lot like soccer, only much bigger.

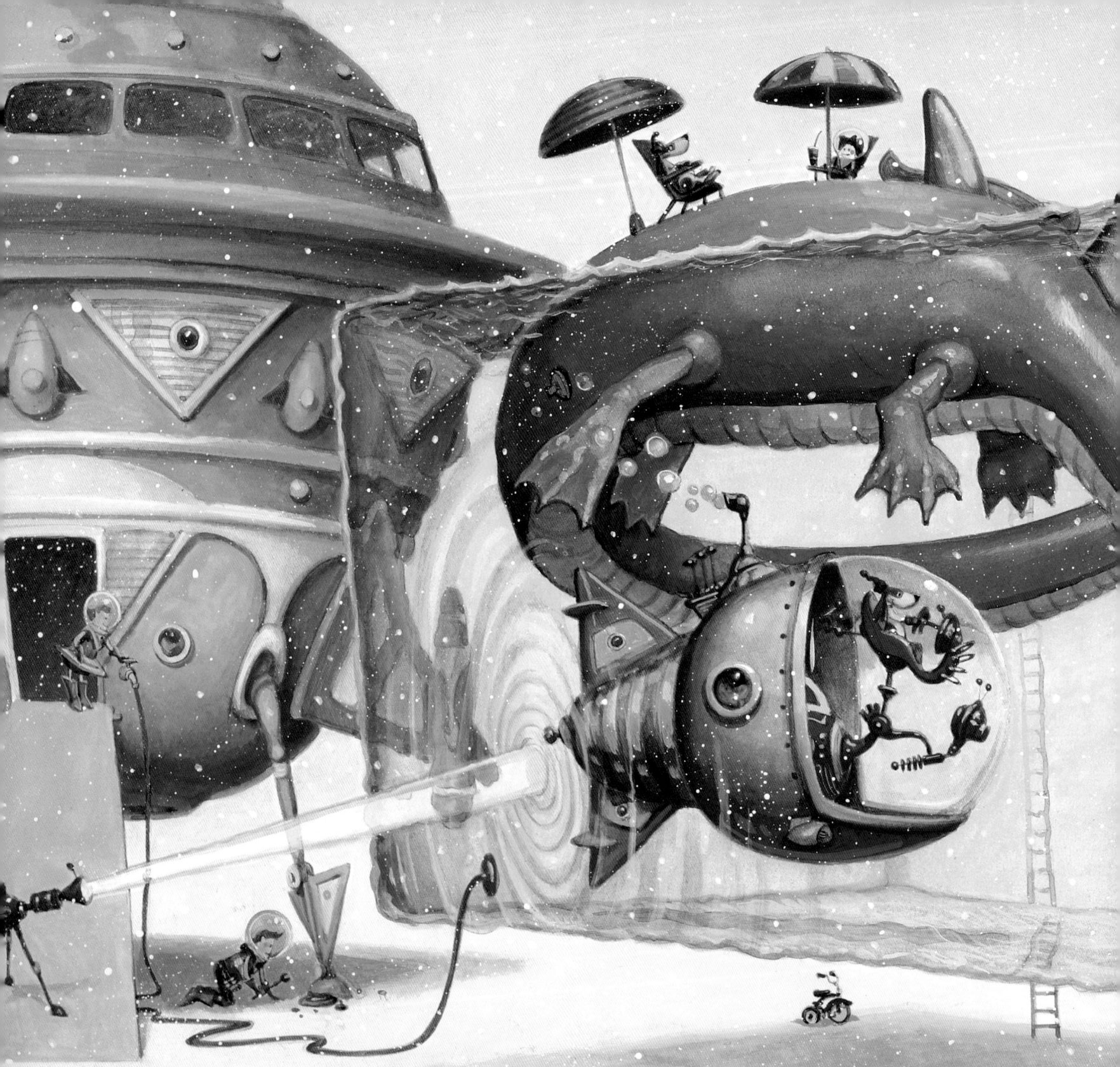

After the game, the space mom set up a force-field swimming pool for the kids, while the space dad inspected their space cruiser for takeoff.

Swimming made Zoomer hungry, and when he got out of the pool in search of a snack, he saw the space dad shaking his head.

"The-saucer-was-damaged-when-it-landed," translated the robot. "It-will-take-weeks-for-a-new-part-to-be-delivered."

Zoomer knew that the family wanted to get home in time for Santa's arrival, so he thought of a solution . . . but it meant giving up his favorite toy.

With Zoomer's trike in place, the spaceship was ready for takeoff. But before they got on board, the space kids gave Hooper, Cooper, and Zoomer something they'd picked up during their travels.

"Wow, thanks!" said Zoomer.

The brothers waved until the spaceship flew out of sight. Then Hooper turned to Zoomer and said, "That was a *really* nice thing you did."

Back home, the boys unwrapped their gift and found the perfect place to display their very own star.

That evening, the earth family ate a wonderful Mom-made dinner. Then the pups hung up their stockings and were hugged and tucked into a warm bed.

Early the next morning, the pups couldn't wait to see if Santa had stopped by.

Hooper received a robot, Cooper a Viking ship, and Zoomer . . .

a new
bicycle!

And on the handlebars was a note:

"Merry Christmas to all!!"